MAXimum Boy

starring in

THE DAY EVERYTHING TASTED LIKE BROCCOLI

BY DAN GREENBURG
ILLUSTRATIONS BY GREG SWEARINGEN

A Little Apple Paperback

SCHOLASTIC
New York   Toronto   London   Auckland   Sydney
Mexico City   New Delhi   Hong Kong

ISBN 0-439-21945-0

Text copyright © 2001 by Dan Greenburg.
Illustrations copyright © 2001 by Scholastic Inc.

All rights reserved. Published by Scholastic Inc.

SCHOLASTIC, LITTLE APPLE PAPERBACKS, and associated logos are trademarks and/or registered trademarks of Scholastic Inc.

12 11 10 9 8 7 6 5   4 5 6/0

Printed in the U.S.A.
First Scholastic printing, May 2001

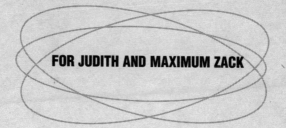

FOR JUDITH AND MAXIMUM ZACK

CHAPTER 1

The President of the United States was on the phone. He seemed pretty excited.

"I have another case for you, Max," he said, "and it's urgent. How soon can you get back to Washington?"

You're probably thinking, why would the President of the United States be asking help from me, Max Silver, an eleven-year-old kid with glasses and braces?

Well, about three years ago at the Air and Space Museum I accidentally handled some glowing blue rocks that had just come back from outer space. Right after that I developed these really weird powers. Like being able to lift a minivan or a steamship over my head. And being able to fly faster than a Stealth bomber. And being able to crush a soda can with one hand. (Actually, I could crush soda cans with one hand *before* handling the space rocks — I'm pretty proud of that.)

If I don't use my superpowers, I'm a really lousy athlete. I'm the second slowest runner in my grade, and the kids hate me when I'm on their relay team. When I use my superpowers I can fly thousands of miles per hour. But if I used my superpowers in school,

I'd blow my cover. You're probably thinking, why don't I use just a *little* of my superpowers, and run maybe *twenty* miles an hour, but that's not how superpowers work. With superpowers, it's all or nothing. I hate that.

I do have a few allergies: Milk products give me a really bad upset stomach. I'm also allergic to sweet potatoes, and certain plants like ragweed make me sneeze my guts out. But my worst allergy is to math. Even *hearing* a math problem is enough to make me pass out or puke. I'm the only kid in the sixth grade with a doctor's excuse to get out of math. Superman had the same trouble with kryptonite.

Anyway, as I said, my real name is Max Silver. I live on the North Side of Chicago, not too far from Lake Michigan, with my mom, my dad, and my teenage sister, Tiffany. The President is always calling me up and asking for my help.

Like now. I had just done a job for him: An evil villain named Dr. Zirkon had disconnected the island of Manhattan, hauled it out to sea, and held it for ransom. I'd beaten Zirkon and pushed Manhattan all the way back to New York. Blah, blah, blah. Big deal. Anyway, the mayor of New York gave me a ticker tape parade, and my family and I had just gotten back to Chicago when the President called and asked me to come to the White House.

"Sir, how soon did you want me back in Washington?" I asked. "Can it wait till after dinner?"

"Only if dinner is a Pop-Tart," said the

President. "Max, you are not going to believe what just happened!"

"If you tell me what happened, sir, I'll probably believe you," I said. "I have never known you to fib."

"That was a figure of speech," said the President. "Max, the governor of California just called. The people of California have suddenly lost their ability to taste food. Whatever they eat tastes exactly like steamed broccoli to them."

"Broccoli?" I said. "Yuck!"

"People are starving," said the President. "Restaurants are deserted. Food stores can't sell groceries. Everything is in chaos. The only things that don't taste like broccoli to them are fried octopus and toothpaste. They've bought up all the octopus and all the

toothpaste in the state, and now panic is starting to set in."

"Octopus?" I said. "Gross!"

"Well, it's not as bad as broccoli," said the President.

I flipped on the TV. An angry-looking crowd of people was outside a grocery store. They were waving their arms, shouting, and throwing rotten vegetables.

"We're coming to you, live, outside a grocery store in Los Angeles, California," a reporter was saying. "What you're seeing is a crowd rioting because the store has run out of both toothpaste and fried octopus."

The picture changed. Another angry-looking crowd of people was in front of a restaurant. They were waving their arms, shouting, and throwing dirty silverware.

"What you're looking at now is a scene in downtown Tijuana, Mexico," said the reporter. "This crowd is angry because this restaurant has no more enchiladas. Somebody in San Diego found that if they go across the California border to Mexico, the enchiladas here still taste like enchiladas. Mobs of people have been crossing the California-Mexico border to eat enchiladas. It's causing complete chaos here in Tijuana."

"Max," said the President on the phone, "I need you to get on this as soon as possible."

I covered the phone and turned to my folks.

"Mom. Dad. The President wants me to start a new case," I said. "Right away. He says I don't have time for dinner."

"But I've made your favorite," said my mom. "Mushroom pizza."

"Well, let me take it with me," I said. "I'll eat it on the way."

"While you're flying, you mean?"

"Yes."

"Max, I've just been handed a bulletin," said the President on the phone. "This broccoli thing is spreading. It's no longer just in California. There are reports it's gotten as far as Nevada, Arizona, and Oregon."

"Oh, boy," I said.

"Max," said my mom, "I do not want you eating while you're flying. I won't have you dripping melted mozzarella all over poor defenseless people in Indiana. It isn't fair."

"I'll be careful, Mom. I promise."

She sighed a loud mom-sigh.

"Well then, take plenty of napkins with you," she said.

CHAPTER 2

A uniformed Marine brought me into the Oval Office, saluted the President, and left. The President was behind his desk. He stood up to shake hands with me.

"Thanks for coming so quickly, Max," said the President. "I'm sorry I had to drag you away from dinner."

"Perfectly all right, sir," I said. "I had

mushroom pizza over Indiana, and a chocolate-chip cookie over Ohio."

"How'd they taste?"

"Delicious, sir."

"I mean did the pizza taste like pizza and the cookie taste like a cookie?"

"Yes, sir."

"You're a very lucky boy. Those poor devils who live in California, Nevada, Arizona, and Oregon aren't so fortunate. To them everything tastes like broccoli. I tell you, Max, it's horrible. Americans have mobbed Mexican restaurants. They're throwing enchilada tantrums in the streets of Tijuana. The President of Mexico has closed the border and threatened war if this goes on."

"Wow," I said. "This *is* serious."

"You bet it is," said the President. "The FBI tells me some supervillain who calls himself the Tastemaker is claiming credit for all this. None of my people have heard of him. Since you're a superhero and all, we thought you'd know him."

"No, sir," I said. "But I do know somebody who might."

"Who's that?" asked the President.

"A superhero named Tortoise Man. I met him at a meeting of the League of Superheroes. He's kind of old and out of shape, but he's really nice. And he lives right here in Washington."

I took out Tortoise Man's business card and showed it to the President. It said: TORTOISE MAN. SUPERHERO, CHAMPION OF THE WEAK, ENEMY OF EVILDOERS EVERYWHERE, HANDYMAN. NO JOB TOO BIG OR TOO SMALL.

BUT NO HEAVY LIFTING, PLEASE. 555-7241.

"Sounds like a good place to start," said the President.

Another Marine escorted me out of the White House, although I could have probably found the way outside by myself. It was a gray December day and the wind was really cold.

"Hey, Maximum Boy!" said a voice behind me.

I turned around. A man in a trench coat walked up to me. He had a big flash camera in his hands and took my picture. The flash kind of hurt my eyes.

"I'm Warren Blatt from the *International Enquirer*," he said. "It's an honor to meet you."

"Thanks," I said.

"I'd like to ask you a couple questions."

"I hate to be rude, sir, but I'm in kind of a hurry," I said.

"Another assignment from the President, huh?"

"Sorry. Can't talk about that now."

"It's the thing in California, isn't it?" said Blatt. "The everything-tasting-like-broccoli thing?"

"I'm afraid my mission is kind of secret," I said. "But . . ."

Just then I saw something awful out of the corner of my eye: An out-of-control truck was about to smash through the big plate-glass window of a restaurant and hit a table full of people.

I flew straight toward the truck, grabbed it by the front fenders, and lifted it high into the air just before it hit the restaurant. Then I set it down on the street. The driver staggered out of the truck. Behind me the reporter from the *International Enquirer* was popping flashes like popcorn in a microwave.

"Great work, kid," said Blatt. "By the way, what's your secret identity? Inquiring minds want to know."

"You know I can't tell you that," I said.

"If you tell me, my paper will pay you a million dollars."

Wow, a million dollars! That kind of money would really help my mom and dad and sister, Tiffany. But it would also place them in danger. If criminals knew where my family was, they could kidnap them. Then they could stop me from fighting crime.

"Sorry, sir," I said, "but I'm not interested."

"Look, son. My assignment is to find out

who you really are. If I fail, they'll . . ." He gulped. ". . . If I fail, well, they'll fire me. I got a wife and three little kids at home, see? If I get fired, they'll starve to death. You could prevent that by telling me who you really are."

I felt bad about Blatt's wife and kids starving, I really did. But I couldn't put my own family in danger, either.

"I wish I could help you, sir," I said. "But I can't."

I leaped into the air.

"You heartless little brat!" Blatt called after me. "I'll find out your secret identity, anyway, someday — with you or without you!"

CHAPTER 3

The Washington address Tortoise Man gave me when I called wasn't a house or an apartment. It was a van. A Volkswagen Microbus parked under a bridge. The neighborhood was kind of depressing. There was garbage all over the place. There was a burned-out car a few yards off.

"Well, well, come in, son," said Tortoise Man. He opened the van door and snapped his big turtle shell into place. "I didn't expect you so soon. Seems like you just hung up the phone."

"I would've been here sooner, but a reporter stopped me," I said, stepping into the middle of the van. "To make up the time, I flew here at eight hundred miles per hour."

"Wow," said Tortoise Man. "Even when I was a young superhero, I never crawled faster than five miles per hour. My tortoise shell was so bulky I could scarcely move. Say, you've got to meet the wife. Honey, you home?" he called.

"Right here, dear," said a voice from the front seat. She sat up. "I was just taking a snooze."

"I'd like you to meet a young friend of mine, Sylvia," said Tortoise Man. "His name

is Maximum Boy. Maximum Boy, meet
Tortoise Woman."

We shook hands.

"Can I offer you a bite of dinner?" she
asked. "We had roadkill in orange sauce. It
was quite tasty. There's still a bit left."

"No thanks, I already ate," I said. "He called you Tortoise Woman. Are you a superhero, too?"

"Well, nowadays I'm more a housewife than a superhero," said Tortoise Woman.

"Nonsense," said Tortoise Man. "Tortoise Woman has sent more than her share of evildoers to jail, I can tell you that. She poured cold water on the career of Burny the Human Torch, and let the hot air out of Balloon Man. So, how can we help you?"

"Somebody in California has made everything taste like steamed broccoli," I said. "He calls himself the Tastemaker. Know anybody like that?"

"Yes," said Tortoise Woman. "He's French, and he's something of a mystery. Some say he developed food poisoning at the most expensive restaurant in Paris. And that made him swear revenge against the whole food industry."

"Some say he flunked out of cooking school," said Tortoise Man. "That he turned to a life of crime when a tapioca pudding he was making went terribly wrong."

"Any idea where he hangs out now?"

"Last *I* heard," said Tortoise Woman, "he was using a converted warehouse over in Venice, California. Just below Santa Monica. Say, you weren't thinking of going out there to capture him alone, were you, dear?"

"Well, that's pretty much what the President asked me to do."

"The Tastemaker is a very dangerous fellow," said Tortoise Man. "Policemen he's tangled with have ended up thinly sliced, deep-fried, or baked in a pie. And I heard he's got some pretty nasty friends. Why don't I come with you?"

"I thought you were pretty much retired," I said.

"Well, it's true I'm more a handyman than a superhero these days. But I can't let a boy your age go after a character like that alone."

"Oh, Porter," said Tortoise Woman. "Maximum Boy doesn't need you. You'd just slow him down."

"Thanks for the offer, sir," I said. "But I can take care of myself."

I talk a lot braver than I feel.

CHAPTER 4

When I left Tortoise Man and Tortoise Woman, I jumped into the air and started flying due west. Over Nebraska I followed the tracks of the Atcheson, Topeka and Santa Fe Railroad for a while. Suddenly, my Maximum vision picked up something awful way below me.

A guy in a wheelchair was crossing the railroad tracks and got stuck. He was trying to free himself, and that's when he saw what *I* saw: A freight train was speeding right toward him. The poor guy was trapped. I zoomed down. Just before it hit him, I lifted the whole train into the air and put it down on the other side of the guy. The guy in the wheelchair thanked me all over the place. But the engineer of the train yelled and shook his fist as I took off. Oh, well, you can't please everybody. Which is one reason being a superhero isn't all that great.

Over Arizona I flew through the Grand Canyon. I always love going through the canyon, swooping down low and looking at the shades of red and purple in the rocks.

Passing over Nevada, I saw crowds of people in the streets of downtown Las Vegas. They seemed to be chanting something. I swooped lower to hear what they were chanting. What they were chanting was, "What do we want? Toothpaste and octopus! When do we want it? Now!" I flew on.

I got to Los Angeles around sunset, sped toward the ocean right over the freeway, turned left at Santa Monica, and landed in Venice. Many years ago, the people of Venice, California, built canals through their town to look like the ones in Venice, Italy. It's pretty cool, but I like the ones in Italy better. I've never been to the Venice in Italy on vacation, but I have been there a couple times on business for the President.

It was already dark by the time I found a warehouse that looked like the one that Tortoise Man and Tortoise Woman described. It was big. And creepy-looking. Rusting metal walls. No windows. Surrounded by a hurricane fence topped with rolls of razor wire. Inside I heard the barking of guard dogs.

I leaped over the fence and rang the doorbell. At first there was no answer. I rang again. The barking of the dogs got louder. Then the huge, heavy door creaked open. It was pretty dark inside, but I could see a guy standing in the doorway. He wore a tuxedo. His hair was shiny and parted in the middle. He had a skinny mustache and a head the size of a watermelon.

The dogs were going crazy. They were barking and baring their teeth.

I growled loudly. They looked startled and backed away.

"May I help you?" asked the guy with the watermelon-sized head.

"Who are you?" I asked.

"The Head Waiter. And what is your name?"

"Maximum Boy. May I come in?"

"Do you have a reservation?"

"A reservation? Uh, no. I'm here to see the Tastemaker."

"I'm sorry. If you have no reservation, you may not come in."

He started to close the door. I held it open with my foot.

He pushed me roughly on the chest. I grabbed his hand and squeezed it so hard I heard something snap inside of it. He gasped at the pain.

"Sorry I had to do that," I said. "After I leave, get an ice pack and put it on that hand for about thirty minutes. And now, let me see the Tastemaker."

"Never!" said the Head Waiter.

"Eet ees all right, Egon," said a voice behind him. It sounded like a French accent, but I wasn't sure.

A man stepped out of the shadows. He flipped a switch and the entire warehouse was suddenly awfully bright. The man was very tall and very skinny. He was dressed in a white chef's outfit, a tall white chef's hat, and a white mask. He had no hands. Where his hands should have been were a steel soup ladle and a meat cleaver.

"I am ze Tastemaker," he said. "To what do I owe ze honor of a visit from ze great Moximum Boy?"

I stepped inside the warehouse. It was an amazing place. It was painted this very bright shiny white color. There were huge, stainless steel machines for making food.

Giant blenders and mixers and stuff. A wide conveyor belt ran from one corner of the warehouse to the other. Dozens of carving knives and meat cleavers hung on the walls. Baskets of rotting fruit and vegetables covered the floor.

"I'm here to make a citizen's arrest," I said. I grabbed the Tastemaker firmly by the arm.

"Ho-ho!" said the Tastemaker. "And for wheech crime do you make such an arrest?"

"The crime of making everything in California, Arizona, Nevada, and Oregon taste like steamed broccoli."

The Tastemaker burst out laughing.

"First," he said when he stopped laughing, "I do not make ze food taste like ze steamed broccoli. And even eef I deed, thees ees not against ze law."

I grabbed his pinky finger and started bending it backward. The Tastemaker squealed like a little girl.

"Stop eet! Stop eet!" he shrieked.

"If I stop, will you tell me the truth?"

"Yais! Yais! Owww!"

I released his pinky finger.

"Zat really *hurt*," he said. "You deed not have to *hurt* me."

"Tell me the truth or I'll do it again."

"OK, *OK*," he said.

"I'm waiting," I said. "Tell me how you made everything taste like broccoli."

"Seemple," he said. "I eenvent a machine called ze Brain Poacher. Eet tune een on ze frequency of human brain waves. Eet reach ze part of ze people's brains zat affect taste — right next to ze hippocampus — and zen I tune eet to STEAMED BROCCOLI. Do you know what ees ze hippocampus?"

"Sure."

"What ees eet?"

"It's, uh, where hippos go to college."

"Wrong!" shouted the Tastemaker. "How do you not know what ees ze hippocampus?"

"Hey, I'm in sixth grade," I said. "Give me a break."

"Well, anyway, zat ees how I control what ze people taste."

"You fiend," I said. "Now nobody in California, Arizona, Nevada, or Oregon can taste anything but steamed broccoli."

He chuckled.

"Oh, eet has gone way past zat by now," he said. "*Way* past. At zis moment eet ees nationwide. No one een ze entire United States has escaped eet. By midnight, eet will have spread over all of North America. By tomorrow, ze world! And zere ees notheeng you can do about eet, either!"

He suddenly chopped at my head with his meat-cleaver hand. I ducked just in time and slammed him up against the wall.

"Maximum Boy," said a voice behind me. It was the Head Waiter. "Your table is ready!" he said.

I turned, just as a table flew through the air and hit me in the chest. I smashed the table into toothpicks. Then I punched the Head Waiter in the stomach. He gasped and dropped to the floor.

The Tastemaker chopped at me again with his cleaver hand. Again, I ducked just in time. The blade of his cleaver stuck in the

wall. Then I focused my laser vision on the metal blade of his cleaver. In a moment it turned bright orange. He yelped with pain. He pulled it out of the wall and stuck it in a bowl of cold soup. It hissed. I grabbed the Tastemaker by the ear and twisted.

"Take me to the Brain Poacher," I said.

"Ow!" said the Tastemaker. "Zat *hurts*!"

"It's supposed to," I said.

The Tastemaker led me to the Brain Poacher. It was huge. It looked like a combination computer and stereo, with lots of lit-up dials and gauges. Behind the machine, wheels spun. Stainless steel pistons went up and down. The machine made a sound I'd never heard before: *TA-POCKETA-POCKETA-POCKETA*. Twin towers of steel rose above the machine. Between the twin towers at the top, long blue sparks crackled and snapped.

"Now dial up the brain-wave frequency and tune in to the taste centers," I said.

He did what I told him to do.

"Now cancel the broccoli wave," I said.

He did that, too.

"Now shut down the whole machine."

He sighed. He turned off switches. He pulled out plugs. He yanked wires out of outlets. The big machine was shutting down. The lights blinked off. The wheels stopped spinning. The pistons stopped going up and down. The *TA-POCKETA-POCKETA-POCKETA* sound stopped. The crackle and snap of the blue sparks at the top of the twin towers stopped, too. The big Brain Poacher machine was silent.

"Is it done?" I asked.

He nodded.

"Eet ees done," he answered sadly. "Eet ees ruined. All my good work. All my beautiful work ees ruined."

"Give me a phone," I said.

He handed me a phone.

"Oh, uh, it's long distance," I said. "If you like I could call collect. . . ."

The Tastemaker waved his hand in disgust and sighed.

"Just dial direct," he said.

I dialed my folks in Chicago. My mom answered.

"Hi, Mom," I said.

"Max, where are you? Are you all right, dear?"

"Yeah," I said. "Perfect. Tell me something. Earlier tonight did anything you ate taste like broccoli?"

"Well, yes, now that you mention it. There was an apple that tasted like broccoli. Also everything at dinner did, too. How did you know that?"

"Do me a favor, Mom. Eat something now. Anything. It doesn't matter what."

"Why?"

"Just do it, please, OK?"

"OK. Here's a banana. I'm eating it. *Mmmm*. Oh!"

"What does it taste like?"

"Like a banana."

"Not like broccoli?"

"No."

"Good. Thanks, Mom. That helps me a lot."

"Will you be home soon, dear?"

"Very soon, Mom. Good night."

I hung up. Then I punched the Brain Poacher. Hard. There was a shower of sparks, a little puff of smoke, and a soft popping sound. The machine was now definitely dead. You could see the shape my fist left in the metal.

I turned to the Tastemaker.

"I'm going now," I said. "It's past my bed-time and I have school tomorrow."

"Curse you, Moximum Boy!" snarled the Tastemaker. "I shall make you pay for thees, no matter how long eet takes — I promees you!"

CHAPTER 5

By the time I got back to Chicago it was almost eleven o'clock. My mom and dad hugged me hello. Even my sister, Tiffany, seemed kind of glad to see me.

"The President called to congratulate you, Max," said my dad. "He said everybody in Washington is very proud of you. He said everybody in the country owes you a lot. They're thinking of putting you on a stamp."

"Thanks, Dad," I said. I was really tired, and my hand hurt from punching the Brain Poacher. "I'm kind of tired. I think I'll just go right to bed."

"You're going to *bed*?" said my stupid sister, Tiffany. "You *can't* go to bed. You have to wash the dinner dishes first!"

"But, Tiff, I've been battling evildoers in California. I'm really tired."

"Mom, if *Max* doesn't do the dishes, then *I'm* going to be stuck doing them again. It isn't fair!"

"But Tiffany," said Mom. "Max has been away battling evildoers in Los Angeles — didn't you hear him?"

"Max is *always* away battling evildoers *some*where, and I always end up doing his stupid chores for him. Max's job is washing the dishes and taking out the garbage. My job is drying the dishes and setting the table. When Max was off in the North Atlantic trying to find the stupid island of Manhattan, who do you think had to take out the stupid garbage? *Me*, that's who. It isn't fair! It just isn't fair!"

"All right, all right," I said. "I'll wash the dishes, OK?"

I walked into the kitchen. The dirty dinner dishes were stacked in a sink of cold water. I squirted detergent into the sink. I focused my X-ray vision on the water and got it boiling hot. Then I went into Maximum speed. I speed-drained the sink, speed-rinsed the dishes, then speed-loaded them into the drying rack. I focused my X-ray vision on them again and sizzled them dry. The whole operation took about thirty seconds.

"There," I said. "I even dried them for you. You satisfied now, Tiff?"

"No," said Tiffany. "You're supposed to do it the *normal* way. It's not fair if you get to use your Maximum powers."

I laughed and went to bed.

The next day at school got off to a bad start. My teacher, Miss Mulvahill, took me aside and told me that my absences from school were becoming a really big problem. That surprised me. Miss Mulvahill is one of the few people who knows I'm Maximum Boy.

"Max," she said, "you're just missing too much school. It sets a bad example for the other children. They see you taking time off from school when you're clearly not sick, and they think *they* should be able to take time off from school, too, when they're not sick."

"But Miss Mulvahill, you know what I'm doing when — "

"Yes, yes, of course I know," she said. "Every time you're absent I get a personal phone call from the President of the United States. He calls me so often, we're on a first-name basis. Look, Max, I know what a service you perform for your country. I know you've saved thousands of lives, and possibly even changed the entire course of history. I'm very proud of you. We all are. But the fact is, you're still missing way too much schoolwork. If you keep being absent so often, well . . . as much as I hate to say this, I'm going to have to give you a failing grade."

I couldn't believe it. I mean, what choice do I have when the President asks me to help him out? Could I say, "Sorry, Mr.

President, I can't go and save the people of California, Nevada, Arizona, and Oregon because I have to be in geography class?" I don't think so. The whole thing seemed so unfair.

When the bell rang for lunch I went down to the boys' room in the basement. That was a huge mistake. Because as soon as I got down there I ran into the class bully, Trevor Fartmeister.

Trevor is huge. He weighs about a hundred and eighty pounds. He's thirteen, but he's only in the sixth grade like me. He has a red buzz cut. Half of his left ear is missing. They say an even bigger kid than Trevor bit it off in a fight. I'd like to see what that kid looks like. Normally, any kid named Fartmeister is asking for trouble. When I tell you that nobody makes jokes about Trevor's last name you'll have some idea of how scary he is. The kids I know wouldn't make fun of him if his name was Trevor Pooperscooper.

"Hey, Silver," said Trevor, "who said you could come into my bathroom?"

"I don't need permission to come in here, Fartmeister, and it's not your bathroom."

"Is so."

"Is not."

"Is so."

"Is not," I said. "It's a public bathroom."

"It's a *private* bathroom and I own it. I've got papers to prove it."

"Yeah? Let's see them."

"They're in my locker. If you want to use my bathroom you have to pay me. Ten cents to wash your hands. Fifty cents to pee. And a buck to take a dump."

There's no way you can win an argument with a bully. Bullies don't have to make sense to win an argument. It was a big mistake coming down here. Usually I don't. Usually I can hold it in all day till I go home. It's not so bad if you have to pee. Peeing you can get away with here. If you ever have to take a dump in the boys' bathroom, though, you take your life in your hands. I mean there are no doors on any of the stalls. Kids come by and heckle you and throw wet toilet paper at you, even if they aren't bullies. In the whole six years I've been at this school I've never taken a dump in the school bathroom.

I really had to pee now. Trevor stood between me and the urinals.

"Get out of my way, Fartmeister."

"Make me," he said. He walked toward me till he was about three inches away and put his hands on his hips.

I know what you're probably thinking. You're probably thinking, why don't I just give him a karate chop or snap off his fingers and shove them up his nose? I mean, I'm Maximum Boy, right? I'm a superhero. I've punched out great white sharks. I've towed the entire island of Manhattan halfway across the Atlantic. I've beaten up master criminals who were *grown-ups*. So why am I standing here, letting a thirteen-year-old bully jerk my chain?

Part of the reason is I'm afraid of blowing my cover. If I snapped off Trevor Fartmeister's fingers and shoved them up his nose, people might find out I'm Maximum Boy. Then I'd be in big trouble. So would my family. Bad guys could kidnap my mom or dad or my sister, Tiffany, and hold them for ransom. Bad guys could force me to lay off them in order to get my family back alive. I could never risk that.

Another part of the reason is that Trevor Fartmeister is a bully. And, as much as I hate to admit it, bullies scare the heck out of me.

"You know what you are, Fartmeister?" I said. "A bully. And everybody knows bullies are cowards."

"So if I'm a coward, that means — what? — that I'm afraid of you?"

"Right," I said.

"So if I'm afraid of you," he said, "I'd probably never do *this*." He pushed me.

"Right," I said.

"And I'd certainly never do *this*." He

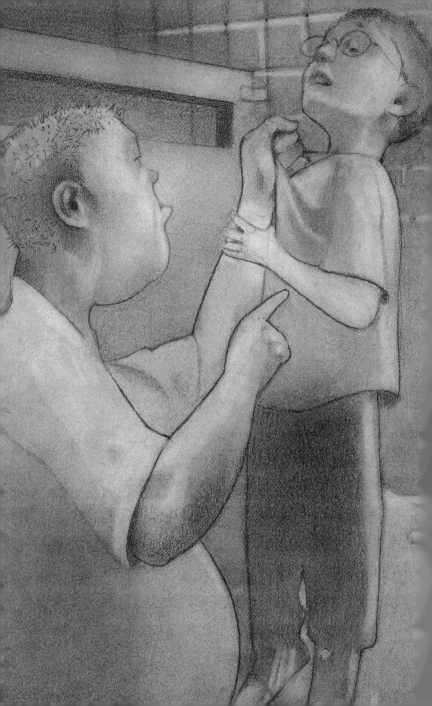

grabbed me by the shirtfront and lifted me off my feet.

"Right," I said.

"And I'd absolutely never *ever* do *this*." He dragged me into one of the stalls and shoved my head into the toilet and flushed.

I'd like to tell you that this was the first swirly I've ever gotten from Trevor Fartmeister. I'd like to tell you that, but if I did, I'd be lying.

Toilet water went up my nose and I practically drowned. Trevor was laughing so hard I thought he'd choke. I wish he had, I mean it. I wished he'd choked and turned blue and dropped dead and rotted on the bathroom floor and stunk the place up.

I went to the sinks and washed my face and hair with plenty of soap from the stupid soap dispenser. Then I dried myself as well as I could with stupid paper towels from the stupid paper towel dispenser. When I left the boys' room, Trevor was still laughing.

I didn't feel like eating lunch anymore, but I went into the cafeteria, anyway.

"What happened to *you*?" said a familiar voice.

It was Charlie Sparks. She's a girl, but she's my best friend. And she's the only kid who knows about my other life.

"I didn't have time to take a shower this morning," I said. "So I washed my hair in the boys' room sink."

"Trevor gave you another swirly, huh?"

I nodded miserably.

"Max, why do you take that from him? Why don't you put your fist right through that fat belly of his till it comes out his back?"

"I'd like to," I said. "But I can't."

"Because you'd blow your cover," she said. "I know. But it would be worth it."

I nodded. We both took trays and got in the lunch line. As usual, there wasn't much to choose from. The special of the day was flat pieces of gray meat floating in brown glue.

"Mystery meat again," said Charlie. "I can't stand the way it tastes."

"Me, either," I said. "Even steamed broccoli tastes better."

She giggled.

"So what happened in Los Angeles, Max? Tell me everything."

"*Sssssshhh,*" I said, looking around.

"C'mon," she insisted. "You gotta tell me. How did the Tastemaker make everything taste like broccoli?"

"Well," I said, "he invented a machine he called the Brain Poacher. . . ." I told her how it worked.

We sat down at a table and started to eat. But the first bite of mystery meat tasted even worse than usual. It tasted like . . . it tasted like cough medicine. I spit it out on my plate.

"Charlie, taste the meat."

"If it's that bad, I don't think I want to."

"No, do me a favor. Taste it."

She shrugged. She cut off a tiny piece of mystery meat. She put it in her mouth. She chewed. She made a face. She spit it out.

"*Phoooo!*" she said. "That's horrible!"

"I know, but what does it taste like?"

"It tastes like . . . cough medicine!"

"That's what I thought," I said.

I looked around me. All over the cafeteria, kids were spitting out their food.

At first, I couldn't figure out what was going on. And then I could. It was the Tastemaker. He'd somehow fixed the Brain Poacher and tuned it to make everything taste like cough medicine!

My beeper went off. I took it off my belt and read the number. Just as I thought, it was the White House.

"Charlie, can you do me a favor?" I said.

"Anything, Max."

I stood up.

"Tell Miss Mulvahill I won't be in class this afternoon. Tell her somebody will call her and tell her why. Get the homework assignment for tonight and tell my folks."

"Where are you going?"

"Back to California."

She looked sad and worried.

"Now do *me* a favor, Max."

"Anything, Charlie."

"Don't let that Tastemaker give you any swirlies."

CHAPTER 6

I put on my Maximum Boy costume in a Mobil gas station rest room. Then I leaped into the air. I didn't go through the Grand Canyon this time. I cut right across the country and flew straight to the Taste-maker's warehouse in Venice. I nearly side-swiped Continental flight 365, American flight 448, a single-engine Piper Cub, and thirty-seven seagulls. It took twenty-four minutes.

This time I didn't bother to ring the doorbell. I tore off the doorknob, pushed my hand through the hole, and twisted the lock tumblers. Then I opened the door and stepped inside the warehouse.

Behind me I heard a floorboard creak. I whirled around in time to get a face full of something hot and mushy — sweet potatoes. Sweet potatoes — yuck! I'm really allergic to sweet potatoes. The Tastemaker scooped his ladle hand into a vat and hurled another load at me. More sweet potatoes splattered my face.

"I thought you promised to stop using the Brain Poacher!" I shouted. "I thought you promised to stop messing around with people's taste!"

"I promees only to stop food tasting like ze broccoli!" answered the Tastemaker. "I promees notheeng about making eet taste like ze coughing medicine!"

Under the table were baskets of rotting fruit and vegetables — tomatoes, peaches, strawberries. Gagging at the sweet potatoes, I started throwing squooshy rotting food at the Tastemaker as fast as I could. I scored lots of direct hits, but the sweet potatoes were beginning to take their toll. I was nauseous and itching all over.

Now the Tastemaker aimed a huge can of whipped cream right at my face and sprayed. My nose and mouth were choked with whipped cream. As allergic as I am to sweet potatoes, it's nothing compared to what milk products like whipped cream do to me.

"Geev up, Maximum Boy!" shouted the Tastemaker. "Geev up or else!"

"Or else what?"

The Tastemaker pointed upward. I looked. The Tastemaker had Tortoise Man chained up and hanging over a huge vat of boiling water. He was waving his arms and legs helplessly.

"Geev up immediately," said the Tastemaker, "or your friend Tortoise Man becomes ze turtle soup!"

If I surrendered to the Tastemaker, then who would stop every bit of food in the country from tasting like cough medicine? Poor Tortoise Man. He looked so helpless. I couldn't let him become turtle soup.

"OK, Tastemaker," I said. "If you promise to let Tortoise Man go free, I'll give up."

"Good," said the Tastemaker.

"But only if you promise on your word of honor."

"Fine."

"Say it," I insisted. "Say 'I promise on my word of honor I will let Tortoise Man go free.'"

"I promees on my word of honor I weel let Tortoise Man go free," the Tastemaker repeated.

"OK," I said. I held out my hands. The Tastemaker tied my wrists together with butcher's twine.

"Now let Tortoise Man go free."

"Uhhhhh . . . no," said the Tastemaker.

I couldn't believe what I was hearing.

"But you *promised*," I said.

"My fingers were crossed, so eet does not count," said the Tastemaker.

"You promised on your word of *honor*," I said.

"I *have* no honor, you fool!" said the Tastemaker.

I was furious. I snapped the butcher's twine and threw it on the floor.

"Two trains speed toward each other!" the Tastemaker shouted. "One of zem ees going ninety miles an hour, one ees going eighty-five! Eef ze trains were thirty miles apart when zey started, how long will eet take zem to collide?"

A math problem! I got so dizzy I could hardly stand. Weakly, I sank to my knees. "H-how d-did you know about my math thing?" I gasped.

The Tastemaker roared with laughter.

"Last night, at a meeting of ze League of

Evil Villains," he answered, "Dr. Zirkon was kind enough to tell us all about eet."

"Zirkon! He's alive? But that's impossible!" I said. "Last time I saw him was underwater in the Atlantic Ocean. He and his assistant, Nobblock, were about to be eaten by a giant octopus!"

The Tastemaker chuckled.

"Oh, do not worry, Dr. Zirkon ees quite healthy. And so ees Nobblock. Tell me, Moximum Boy, what ees ze square root of 129?"

"Aaarrgh!" I croaked. Then everything went black.

CHAPTER 7

I awoke to the feeling that I couldn't move. I opened my eyes. My wrists and ankles were chained to a wide, industrial-sized rubber conveyor belt. Attached to the conveyor belt, on a bracket above my head, was a huge electronic signboard with flashing letters. It said: IF ALICE CAN WASH THIRTY-ONE DISHES IN SEVEN MINUTES, AND MARY CAN WASH TWENTY-EIGHT DISHES IN THREE MINUTES,

AND NAOMI CAN WASH THIRTY-THREE DISHES IN FOUR MINUTES, HOW LONG WILL IT TAKE ALL THREE GIRLS TO WASH ONE HUNDRED DISHES AFTER DINNER?

I suddenly got so weak I could hardly breathe. Also, I felt like hurling.

"This is all my fault, kid," said a sad voice. It was Tortoise Man. He was chained to the conveyor belt right next to me. "None of this would have happened if I hadn't tried to be a superhero. I thought I could help you by coming out here. But the Tastemaker was too fast for me. Also, I'm kind of a klutz."

"How'd you get out here?" I asked.

"On an airliner, how do you think? The wife and I had a lot of frequent-flier miles saved up over the years. This never would have happened to me in the old days."

"You were faster then?"

"Truthfully, no. I never hit top speeds of more than five miles per hour. But it's my fault we're locked up like this."

"No it's not," I said miserably. "It's *my* fault for being totally wiped out every time I hear or see a math problem. What a dork I am!"

"Nonsense," said Tortoise Man. "You're no more a dork than I am."

"Well, I'm just so ashamed of what math problems do to me."

"Don't be so hard on yourself," said Tortoise Man. "Remember, Superman is totally wiped out by kryptonite."

"I know," I answered. "And that doesn't even make any sense. I mean why would a tiny *piece* of kryptonite wipe out Superman? Before he came to Earth, when he was still on the planet Krypton — which is *solid* kryptonite — he had normal powers, right? I mean, I just don't get it."

Tortoise Man was quiet for a while. "You know," he said, "I used to produce a special Tortoise Ray that caused evildoers to go into slow motion."

"Really?"

"Yes," he said. "It wasn't anything flashy, like most superheroes have, but it was mine. It used to slow supervillains down to my speed so I could have a go at them. It worked pretty well. Years ago, there was a villain who called himself the March Hare. He'd race through a crowd of people and pick their pockets so fast they wouldn't even know it. My Tortoise Ray slowed him way down."

"Slow enough for you to catch him, huh?"

"Oh, no," he said. "Not *that* slow — I mean I go five miles per hour, *tops*. But slow enough for the people whose pockets he picked to smack him in the face and save their wallets. And slow enough for the cops to catch him and throw him in jail. I wonder if I could still do it. I haven't tried it in years. It's something you have to keep practicing. Like scales on the piano."

The Tastemaker walked over to the conveyor belt.

"So, gentlemen, you have had ze nice snooze?"

"Let us go, you fiend," I said.

"And why would I do zat?"

"Because you promised to on your word of honor."

"No, no, I deed not. I promees only to let Tubby ze Turtle go."

"Then do it."

"But I change my mind. I take back ze promees."

"A promise is a promise. You can't just take it back, you miserable liar."

"*Tsk, tsk, tsk,*" said the Tastemaker. "Such a temper you have, Moximum Boy. Tell me. Who do you theenk you are?"

"What do you mean?"

"I mean I weesh to know who you are. What ees your secret identity? Ze *International Enquirer* offers one million dollars to know, and I need ze money."

"You'll have to kill me to find out."

The Tastemaker laughed.

"Zat I am going to do anyway," he said.

"So what now, Tastemaker?" asked Tortoise Man. "First you make all food taste like broccoli. Then you make it taste like cough medicine. What are you going to make food taste like next — stinky cheese?"

"Oh, no, no. My next plan ees some-theeng much more ambitious. I am ready for ze final phase. I no longer weesh to change what food tastes like to people. Now I weesh to change what *people* taste like."

"What?"

"My new sausage-making machine weel turn people eento food. Tasty leettle gourmet sausages, wrapped een pancakes, with ze nice hickory-smoked taste. Human pigs-een-blankets. *Mmmmm*. How sad zat you weel not be able to taste yourselves before you die. I have just feenished fine-tuning ze machinery. Would you like to see how eet works?"

"No."

"Oh, *tsk, tsk*, what a pity."

"How are you going to get people to come to your sausage-making machine?" I asked.

"Weeth ze Brain Poacher," he said. "I weel set ze frequency zat makes zem come here to ze warehouse. Do not worry — zey weel come."

The Tastemaker threw a switch. I heard the sound of motors beginning to hum.

"And now I show you how ze sausage-maker works."

He threw a second switch. At the other end of the conveyor belt, the razor-sharp jaws of the sausage grinder started up. They made an awful grinding noise. He threw a third switch. The conveyor belt jerked into motion. Tortoise Man and I were on our way to becoming pigs-in-blankets.

CHAPTER 8

The conveyor belt moved slowly but steadily toward the sausage grinder. I tried to break the steel chains that held my wrists and ankles. It was hopeless. I was as weak as a newborn kitten. Above me was another flashing sign: SAM WAS BORN ON HIS FATHER'S THIRTIETH BIRTHDAY. SAM'S FATHER IS SIX YEARS MORE THAN THREE TIMES SAM'S AGE. HOW OLD ARE SAM AND HIS FATHER NOW?

Aaaaarrrggghh! I hiccuped and belched at the same time.

Now we were twenty feet from the sausage grinder . . . now nineteen . . . now eighteen . . . The Tastemaker walked along beside us, enjoying our ride. I tried not to see that sign. I tried to not think about Sam and his stupid father.

"So, Maximum Boy," said the Tastemaker. "You weel soon become something truly useful — food."

"What is it with you and food?" I asked.

I closed my eyes so I couldn't see the signs, but my X-ray vision picked one up anyway: A BAG CONTAINS 120 NICKELS AND DIMES WITH A TOTAL VALUE OF TEN DOLLARS. HOW MANY DIMES ARE IN THE BAG?

Aaaaaarrrgghh!

"What ees eet weeth me and food?" the

Tastemaker repeated. "O-ho, zat ees a good one, Moximum Boy! Zat ees really a good one!"

Now we were sixteen feet from the sausage machine . . . now fifteen . . . now fourteen . . .

"Let us say zat a baby ees born without ze sense of taste, eh?" said the Tastemaker. "He have ze sense of sight, ze sense of smell — all of ze senses except ze sense of taste, eh? Let us say zat when ze baby grows eento a leettle boy, hees schoolmates feed heem brown mud and tell heem eet ees chocolate pudding. And zey feed heem long skinny worms and tell heem eet ees spaghetti. And zey feed heem cat poo-poo and tell heem eet ees Tootsie Rolls . . ."

"And that little boy was you?" I asked. I tried to think about something besides that stupid bag full of nickels and dimes. I thought about cat poo-poo and Tootsie Rolls.

Now we were thirteen feet from the sausage machine . . . now twelve . . . now eleven . . .

"And let us say zat leettle boy does not *know* he ees eating worms and mud and cat poo-poo, *because he have no sense of taste. Because to heem everytheeng taste like cardboard.* Do you theenk when zat leettle boy becomes a man he might be a teensy-weensy bit *angry*?"

Now we were ten feet from the sausage machine . . . now nine . . . now eight . . . The math problem was starting to fade from sight, but I still wasn't strong enough to break my chains and tear my wrists off the conveyor belt. I still needed another few seconds to regain my strength. But in another few seconds the razor-sharp jaws of the sausage machine would grind us to bits.

"Do you theenk when zat leettle boy becomes a man he might decide to take revenge on everybody who *has* ze sense of taste? *Do you theenk he might decide to make . . . whatever they ate . . . taste like broccoli . . . or cough medicine . . . or . . . turn . . . zem . . . all . . . eento . . . sausages?*"

Something weird was happening. The Tastemaker had suddenly started slowing down. So had the conveyor belt and the sausage machine. They were hardly moving at all.

"It's working!" said Tortoise Man. "My Tortoise Ray is actually working!"

The conveyor belt was now moving so slowly I had time to get back some of my strength. I took a deep breath. I yanked at

the chains. They stretched. They broke. I got up from the conveyor belt and freed Tortoise Man.

"Thank you, Tortoise Man," I said.

"You're welcome, Maximum Boy."

I turned and slugged the Tastemaker. He hit the floor in slow motion and slowly went unconscious. Then I threw three switches and turned off the conveyor belt and the sausage machine.

CHAPTER 9

After we took the Tastemaker and the Head Waiter to the Los Angeles County Jail, I flew Tortoise Man to Washington and dropped him off at his van. By the time I got home to Chicago, it was almost midnight. My mom and dad were practically jumping out of their skins.

"Max, it's so late," said my mom. "We were worried sick. What happened?"

"Well, Mom, it just took us longer to capture the Tastemaker than we thought."

Dad turned on the TV. A famous newsman — I can't think of his name, but you'd know him if you saw his face — was just finishing up a story.

". . . And so it was that a young boy and a strange, hard-shelled man — Maximum Boy and Tortoise Man — captured the archcriminal who turned all our food into broccoli and put him where he'll have to pay his debt to society. And a grateful nation says, 'Thank you, Maximum Boy. And thank you, too, Tortoise Man.' And now, for me and for the entire Fox News team, good night and good luck."

"Oh, I forgot to tell you," said Dad. "The President called. He heard about the capture. He said to tell you he's very proud of you, son. And so are your mother and I."

"Thanks, Dad."

"I think even Tiffany is proud of you. She just has trouble saying it."

"I know," I said.

"Did you have anything to eat in Los Angeles?" Mom asked.

"Uh, yeah."

"What did you eat?"

"Mostly . . . sweet potatoes and whipped cream."

My mother sighed.

"Max, how are you ever going to grow big and strong if you don't eat a balanced diet?" she asked.

At school the next morning, Miss Mulvahill took me aside for another little talk.

"Max, I think I've been a little too tough on you," she said. "After all, you're not missing school because you're playing hooky. It's because you're doing heroic things to keep our country safe from criminals. So I'm giving you a chance to make up the work you miss while you're on missions for the President."

"Thank you, Miss Mulvahill," I said. "That's terrific."

"I've arranged for a private tutor who'll work with you every Saturday and Sunday at your home."

"Uh, you mean I'm going to have school now seven days a week instead of five?"

"That's right, Max."

"Oh, *great*," I said.

"I *knew* you'd be pleased," said Miss Mulvahill.

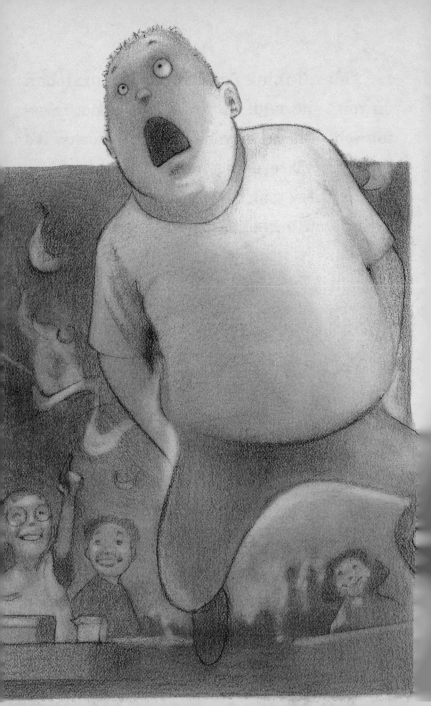

At lunch, Charlie loved hearing how Tortoise Man and I beat the Tastemaker. While I was telling her the story, we saw Trevor Fartmeister come into the cafeteria. He sat down on the metal railing that separates the lunch line from the tables and started hassling one of the kids in the lunch line.

"That Trevor is such a dork," said Charlie. "If only there was some way you could use your powers on him without blowing your cover."

"Yeah."

I watched Trevor sitting on the metal railing and hassling the poor kid in the lunch line.

"You know something?" I said. "Maybe there is."

I focused my X-ray vision on the metal

railing. In two seconds it turned red-hot.

Trevor's eyes almost popped out of their sockets. Screaming like a banshee, he tore out of the cafeteria. The seat of Trevor's pants was *smoking*.

So, anyway, that's the story of the day everything started tasting like broccoli. And it looked like I was finally going to be able to go to school without having to rush off on missions from the President. Until this thing that just happened to me, I mean. Let me tell you about it.

Check out this sneak preview from the next nail-biting Maximum Boy Adventure!

SUPERHERO . . . OR SUPER THIEF?

"Well, Max?" said the President.

"Sir, I don't understand this," I said. "I didn't steal that painting."

"No? I will now show you the next tape," said the President. "This one is from the Tower of London in England."

He put in the next tape. Two Royal Beefeater guards, dressed in red uniforms and black hats, stood guarding a table. A lot of people were standing around, admiring what was on the table. The table was covered with a purple velvet cloth. On top of the purple velvet cloth was a glass case. Inside the glass case were a gold crown and a lot of diamonds and rubies and emeralds and stuff. Suddenly, the people and the guards froze. Then a kid dressed in a black baseball uniform and a silver cape raced in, took the crown and the jewels out of the case, and raced off. The kid sure looked like me.

"Do you have anything to say *now*, Max?" asked the President.

"Sir, I did not steal the Crown Jewels," I said.

"Is that so?" said the President. "The next tape is from Fort Knox, Kentucky."

This tape showed a huge stack of gold bars. Soldiers with rifles marched back and forth in front of the stack of gold bars. Suddenly, the marching guards froze in mid-step. A kid in a black baseball uniform and a silver cape rolled a wheelbarrow up to the stack of gold bars. Boy, did he ever look like me! He filled the wheelbarrow full of gold, then rolled it away.

"And what about now?" asked the President. . . .

"Sir, I did not steal the beef bouillon," I said.

"*Gold* bullion," said the President.

"Whatever. I did not steal it." . . .

"Max," said the President, "don't lie to me. I saw the same tapes you did. It's pretty clear to me who stole those treasures. And I wouldn't be at all surprised to learn your friend Tortoise Man helped you do it. I want you to go home now and think about what you did. Then I want you to come back and tell me what we should do with you."

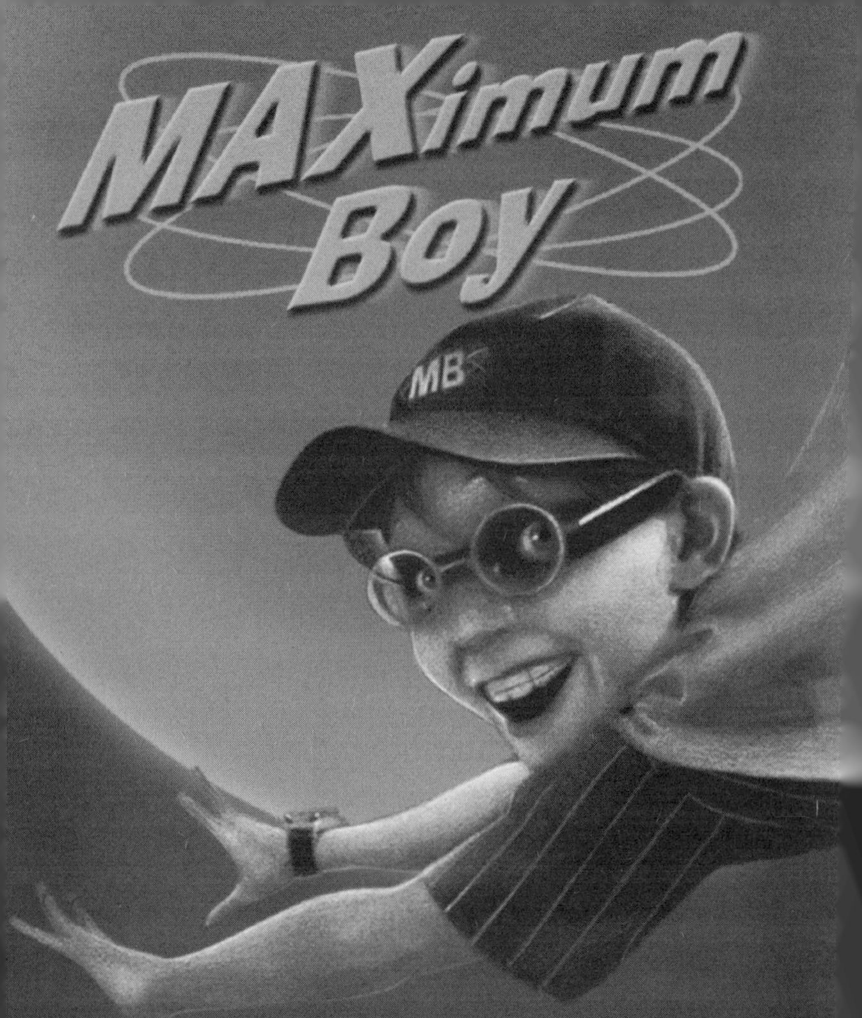
MAXimum Boy
MB